Dear Parents,

Welcome to the Scholastic Reader series. We have taken over 80 years of experience with teachers, parents, and children and put it into a program that is designed to match your child's interests and skills.

Level 1—Short sentences and stories made up of words kids can sound out using their phonics skills and words that are important to remember.

Level 2—Longer sentences and stories with words kids need to know and new "big" words that they will want to know.

Level 3—From sentences to paragraphs to longer stories, these books have large "chunks" of texts and are made up of a rich vocabulary.

Level 4—First chapter books with more words and fewer pictures.

It is important that children learn to read well enough to succeed in school and beyond. Here are ideas for reading this book with your child:

- Look at the book together. Encourage your child to read the title and make a prediction about the story.
- Read the book together. Encourage your child to sound out words when appropriate. When your child struggles, you can help by providing the word.
- Encourage your child to retell the story. This is a great way to check for comprehension.
- Have your child take the fluency test on the last page to check progress.

Scholastic Readers are designed to support your child's efforts to learn how to read at every age and every stage. Enjoy helping your child learn to read and love to read.

—Francie Alexander
Chief Education Offi
Scholastic Education

Compilation Copyright © 1999 by David McPhail.
A Bug, a Bear, and a Boy Go to School; A Bug, a Bear, and a Boy Go for a Ride;
A Bug, a Bear, and a Boy Fly a Kite; A Bug, a Bear, and a Boy Paint a Picture
Copyright © 1998 by David McPhail.
Activities copyright © 2003 Scholastic Inc.

Library of Congress Cataloging-in-Publication Data is available.

ISBN 0-439-07783-4

10 9 8 7 6   06 07
Printed in the U.S.A.   23
First printing, September 1999

A Bug, a Bear, and a Boy Go to School

by David McPhail

Scholastic Reader — Level 1

SCHOLASTIC INC. Cartwheel B·O·O·K·S ®

New York   Toronto   London   Auckland   Sydney
Mexico City   New Delhi   Hong Kong   Buenos Aires

School

A bug, a boy, and a bear
go to school.
The bear carries the books.

The boy carries the pencils
and paper.
The bug carries the eraser.

They write their names
on the blackboard.
The bear writes his name
at the top.
The boy writes his name
in the middle.
The bug writes his name
at the bottom.

They look at the globe.
The bear points to the North Pole.
The bug points to the South Pole.
The boy points to the equator.

Outside they try to seesaw,
but the bear is too big.

So they swing instead.

Best of all, they read.

The Ride

The bear wants to go for a ride.
He sits in the wagon.

The boy pulls.
The bug pushes.

The wagon does not move.
The bear is too big.

This time, the bug pulls
and the boy pushes.

The wagon still does not move.
The bear has an idea.

He gets out of the wagon.

He pulls it to the top of a hill.

Then he gets back in.
The bug and the boy get in, too.

They all go for a ride.

The Kite

A boy, a bug, and a bear
want to fly a kite.

They take the kite outside.
The kite will not fly.
It falls to the ground.

It needs a tail.
"I will be the tail," says the bug.

The bug holds on to the kite.
Now it flies.

The wind takes the kite
high in the air.

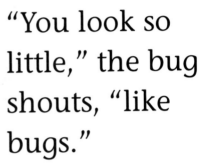

"You look so
little," the bug
shouts, "like
bugs."

The wind dies.
The boy and the bear pull
the kite back to earth.

"You don't
look like bugs
anymore,"
says the bug.
They all
laugh.

The Picture

The bug, the boy, and the bear
want to paint a picture.

The bear has a big brush.
He paints something big.

The boy's brush is not
as big as the bear's.
He paints something smaller.

The bug has a tiny brush.
He paints something smaller.

They paint for a long time.

The bear hangs the picture
on the wall.

Then the bug, the bear,
and the boy sit down
to look at it.

They are pleased.